OL' BLOO'S
BOOGIE-WOOGIE BAND
AND BLUES ENSEMBLE

Jan Huling

Illustrated by
Henri Sørensen

Ω
PEACHTREE
ATLANTA

To the one and only Brattleboro Boogie-Woogie

Band and Blues Ensemble. We was great.

—J. H.

For Lise Winther

—H. S.

Ω

Published by
PEACHTREE PUBLISHERS
1700 Chattahoochee Avenue
Atlanta, Georgia 30318-2112

www.peachtree-online.com

Text © 2010 by Jan Huling
Illustrations © 2010 by Henri Sørensen

Book design by Loraine M. Joyner
Illustrations created in oil on canvas. Title typeset in Nick Curtis's Boogie Nights; text typeset in Palatino Infant Roman.

Printed and manufactured in March 2010 by Imago in Singapore
10 9 8 7 6 5 4 3 2 1

First Edition

Library of Congress Cataloging in Publication Data
Huling, Jan.
 Ol' Bloo's boogie-woogie band and blues ensemble / written by Jan Huling ; illustrated by Henri Sørensen.
  p. cm.
 Summary: Set in Louisiana, four aging animals who are no longer of any use to their masters find a new home after outwitting a gang of robbers.
 ISBN 978-1-56145-436-5 / 1-56145-436-2
 [1. Fairy tales. 2. Folklore—Germany.] I. Sorensen, Henri, ill. II. Bremen town musicians. English. III. Title. IV. Title: Old Blue's boogie-woogie band and blues ensemble.
 PZ8.H875Ol 2010
 398.2—dc22
                    2009040520

Once upon a time not so awful long ago, out where the great states of Louisiana and Texas rub shoulders, there lived a farmer who had himself a donkey. Ol' Bloo Donkey spent year after year haulin' cotton, dreamin' of the day he could enjoy a well-earned retirement.

One day, with the sun bakin' the fields, Ol' Bloo Donkey sat his tired self down to rest for a bit. That's when he happened to hear Farmer Brown talkin' to his wife.

"Yeah, you're right, Mama," says the farmer. "Ol' Bloo Donkey's gettin' too decrepit to be of use to us. We can't afford to feed no critter that can't work. I gotta put the poor beast outta his misery."

Ol' Bloo Donkey couldn't believe his long ears. But he sure wasn't gonna wait around to find out if he'd heard right. He was up and gone before ol' Farmer Brown could haul out of his rocker.

Ol' Bloo Donkey trotted down the road, and he didn't stop until the very next day when he sat himself down to make a plan.

"Well now, Farmer Brown had himself a point about me bein'
jest a mite past my prime," says the ol' donkey to himself. "Maybe
I do need a change of career. I've heard them folks down New
Orleans way have a keen appreciation for music. And I do have
me a beee-yooo-ti-ful singin' voice."

With that, he commenced to brayin' and hee-hawin', pleased
as punch at the sound of his own voice. Now, if you can imagine
the sound an accordion makes fallin' down a flight of stairs, you
got some notion of the sound of Ol' Bloo Donkey's singin' voice.

So off he went to seek fame and fortune, hee-hawin' all the way.

Before long, Ol' Bloo Donkey noticed that he wasn't singin'
alone. His beee-yooo-ti-ful solo was now a duet.

"Well, I'll be," he says. "Seems another musician lurks in
yon bushes. Show yerself, O silver-throated varmint!"

Out from behind a blackberry bush lumbered a flea-bit
ol' hound dog, just as matted and nasty as could be.

"Tell me, friend, what're you doin' out here in the middle of no place at all?" asks Ol' Bloo Donkey.

"It's like this," replies Gnarly Dog. "I lived in a house with folks who'd pat me and throw stuff for me to fetch. Then I got old and they got a new pup and they didn't want me around no more."

"That's a sad tale for sure," says Ol' Bloo Donkey. "I'm headin' New Orleans way to sing in a honky-tonk. Why not come with me? Them big city folks won't know what hit 'em!"

So Gnarly Dog—whose voice sounded like a gui-tar bein' scraped with a washboard— and Ol' Bloo Donkey—whose voice sounded like an accordion fallin' down the stairs— continued on down the road, screeching to a boogie-woogie beat.

A few miles on, their duet mysteriously turned into a trio.

"Well, I'll be," declares Ol' Bloo Donkey. "What gentle music is that? Show yerself, O golden-throated varmint!"

Out from the palmettos came a scrawny, half-blind yeller cat lookin' sad and downhearted.

"What're you doin' way out here and why so sad?" Ol' Bloo asks.

"It's like this," says One-Eyed Lemony Cat. "I lived in a cottage with an ol' lady who used to scratch behind my ears and let me eat all the mice I could catch. Then I got on in years, and the ol' gal gave me the boot!"

"Well, me and Gnarly Dog here are headin' to New Orleans to sing in a honky-tonk," Ol' Bloo Donkey says. "Why not come with us? Them big city folks won't know what hit 'em!"

So One-Eyed Lemony Cat—whose voice sounded like a fiddle bein' played with a carvin' knife—and Gnarly Dog—whose voice sounded like a gui-tar bein' scraped with a washboard—and Ol' Bloo Donkey—whose voice sounded like an accordion fallin' down the stairs—continued on down the road, howlin' in a fine blues style.

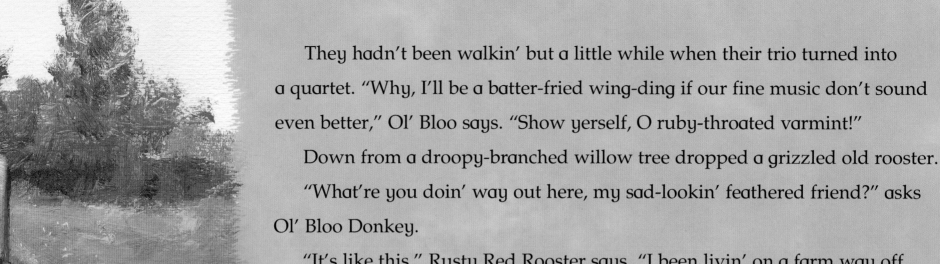

They hadn't been walkin' but a little while when their trio turned into a quartet. "Why, I'll be a batter-fried wing-ding if our fine music don't sound even better," Ol' Bloo says. "Show yerself, O ruby-throated varmint!"

Down from a droopy-branched willow tree dropped a grizzled old rooster.

"What're you doin' way out here, my sad-lookin' feathered friend?" asks Ol' Bloo Donkey.

"It's like this," Rusty Red Rooster says. "I been livin' on a farm way off yonder, ever since I was an egg. Had me a good job, too, wakin' folks up every day. Then one of 'em gets a newfangled alarm clock and I'm outta business!

"Well, we're headed for New Orleans to sing in a honky-tonk," Ol' Bloo Donkey says. "C'mon and join us. Them big city folks won't know what hit 'em!"

So Rusty Red Rooster—whose voice sounded like a player piano bein' hit with an ax—and One-Eyed Lemony Cat—whose voice sounded like a fiddle bein' played with a carvin' knife—and Gnarly Dog—whose voice sounded like a gui-tar bein' scraped with a washboard—and Ol' Bloo Donkey—whose voice sounded like an accordion fallin' down the stairs—marched off, scattin' and beboppin' all the way.

When evenin' settled in, the four friends decided they needed to bed down for the night. They was all tuckered out and right hungry, too, but had nary a morsel between 'em.

"Hey, band!" calls Rusty Red Rooster. "I see a lit-up cabin in yon distance. Let's go see if we can sing for our supper."

They all agreed it was a fine idea and off they went to the cabin.

"Let's have a peek at our first audience," says Gnarly Dog.
So the ragtag band of four tippy-toed to the window.

Inside the cabin they spied a table covered with a banquet the likes of which they'd never seen. There was gumbo and étouffée, muffalettas and po-boys, pralines and bread puddin', and more besides. And sittin' 'round that table were three rough, tough, ugly-lookin' thieves, jest glarin' at one another and pickin' their teeth with their knives.

"Man oh man," whispers One-Eyed Lemony Cat. "They sure don't look like music lovers."

"You never know," says Ol' Bloo Donkey. "Let's get ourselves set up for this here gig."

So Ol' Bloo Donkey stepped up onto a wobbly wooden crate in front of the window, and Gnarly Dog climbed onto his back. One-Eyed Lemony Cat scrambled up onto Gnarly Dog's back, and Rusty Red Rooster flapped up to the top.

They all took a great gulp of air, and then let out the loudest, craziest, awfullest shriek you can possibly imagine. And as they did, that ol' wooden crate caved right in, and all four critters went crashin' through the window and into the cabin!

All that screechin' and crashin' near scared them three thieves half to death.

They screamed like the devil, then hightailed it outta that cabin and fled deep into the woods.

Once the band was back on its many feet and had regained its dignity, the famished musicians couldn't keep from helpin' themselves to all that good food. They ate and ate 'til they were plum wore out and too stuffed to eat any more. "Might as well go to bed, y'all," says Ol' Bloo Donkey.

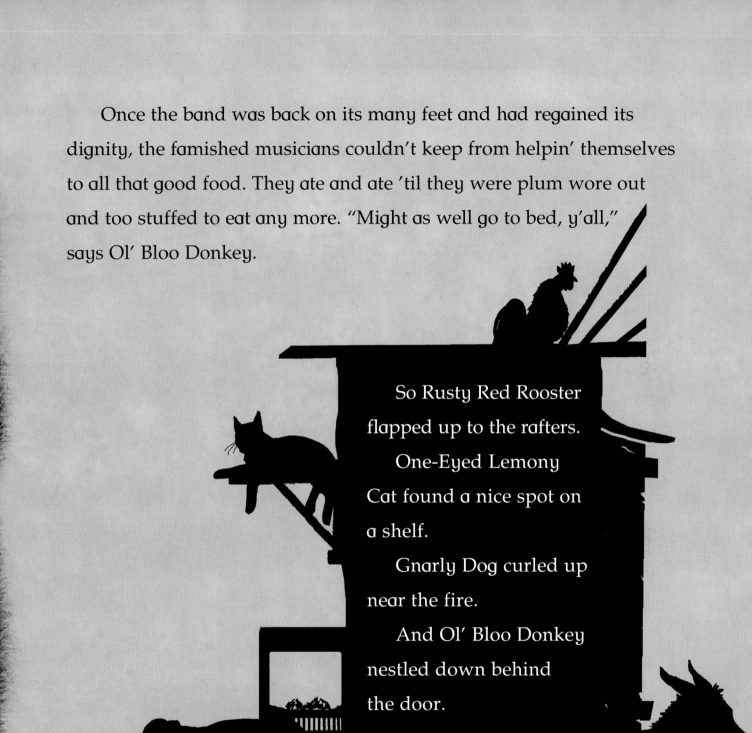

So Rusty Red Rooster flapped up to the rafters.

One-Eyed Lemony Cat found a nice spot on a shelf.

Gnarly Dog curled up near the fire.

And Ol' Bloo Donkey nestled down behind the door.

Soon they were all happily snoozin' and snorin'…

Out in the forest, the three thieves finally stopped their hightailin' and commenced to speculatin'.

"What in tarnation was that?" whimpers one of the thieves.

"A monster sent straight from the Devil himself," says another. "Did you see all them feathers 'n fur 'n teeth? And did you hear that terrible, unholy sound?"

"Well, seems pretty quiet now," says the third thief. "Could be it's gone. I'm headin' back to claim our loot. Who's with me?"

No one answered, so that there thief tightened his belt, straightened his hat, and sneaked back to the cabin all alone.

When he got there, he heard nary a sound. All was dark and still.

He slowly opened the door, crept to the hearth, and found the matches.

With shakin' hands, he finally brought a match to fire right smack

in the one good eye of One-Eyed Lemony Cat!

That yeller feline was so startled,
she shot up all puffed and screechin' and
scratched the thief smartly on the nose!

The match flew to the floor and went out.
The terrified thief stumbled for the door in
the dark and stepped on Gnarly Dog, who
chomped squarely on the offender's leg.

Howlin' like a banshee, the thief ran straight into the path of Ol' Bloo Donkey, who gave him a kick with both hind legs that sent the thief flyin'.

All the while Rusty Red Rooster kept cryin' "COCK-A-DOODLE-DOO!" at the top of his gristly lungs!

That thief took off like a shot and didn't stop runnin' 'til he was deep in the woods.

"It's still there, all right," he tells his colleagues. "And it's even bigger 'n meaner than we thought. That monster had razor-sharp claws and a bear-trap grip. It beat me so hard that all the air went clean outta me. The worstest, blackest nightmare you can imagine. And most terrible of all, the whole time that fiend kept screamin', *'I'm a-gonna git you!'* Let's skedaddle!"

So off went them three thieves, never to be seen nor heard of in those parts again.

Ol' Bloo Donkey, Gnarly Dog,
One-Eyed Lemony Cat, and Rusty
Red Rooster never did get to that
fancy honky-tonk in New Orleans.
The comfy little cabin in the woods
was a right perfect spot to retire, so
there they lived and sang in harmony
for the rest of their days.

Them big city folks never knew what they missed!